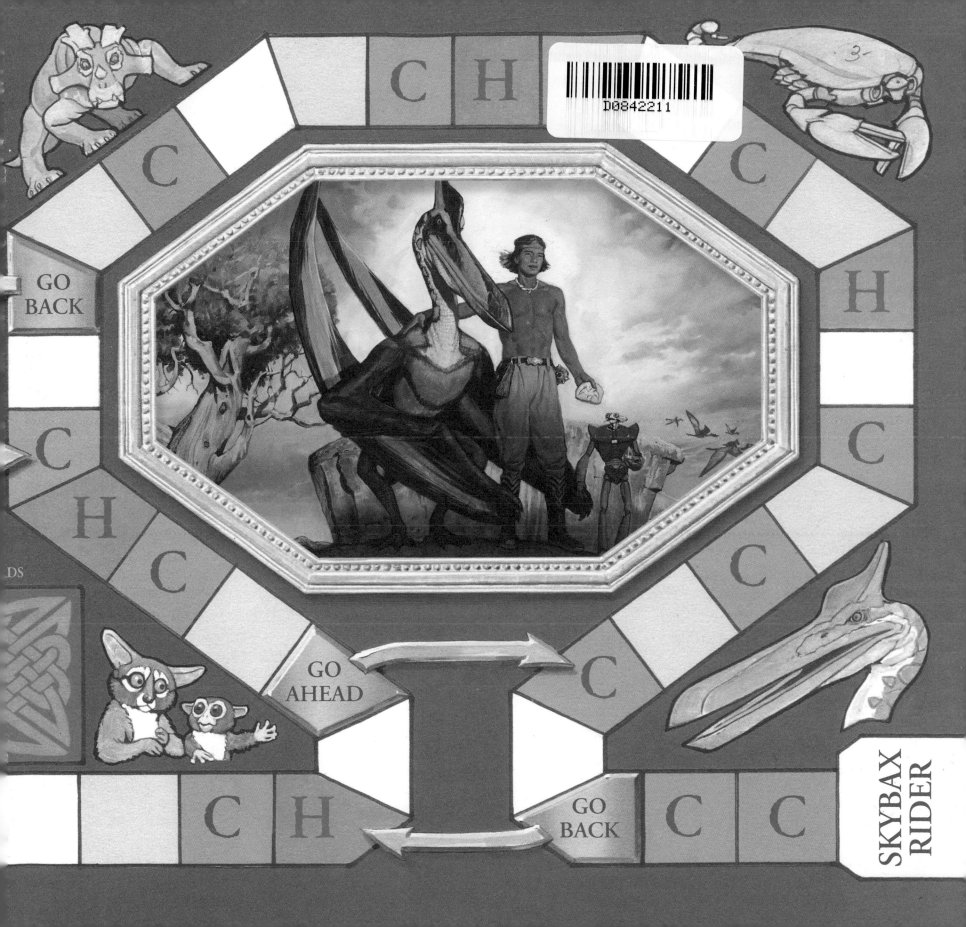

D0842211

SKYBAX RIDER

DINOTOPIA: FIRST FLIGHT

DINOTOPIA: FIRST FLIGHT

Written and Illustrated by James Gurney

HarperCollinsPublishers

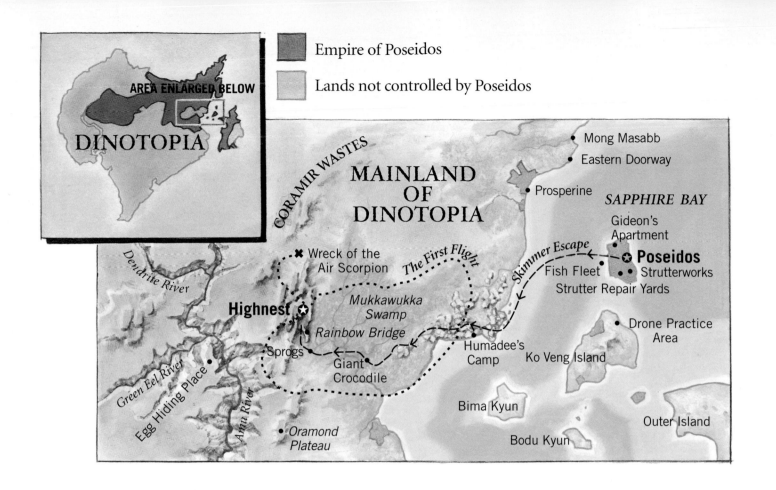

For Jeanette, Dan, and Franklin, my hero partners

With thanks to Michael Stone, Alix Reid, and
Vicki Hickman for their faith in new journeys

Dinotopia: First Flight
Copyright © 1999 by James Gurney
Board game copyright © 1999 by James Gurney
Printed in China. All rights reserved.
LC Number: 99-60932
1 2 3 4 5 6 7 8 9 10
❖
First Edition

Dinotopia is a trademark of James Gurney
Visit Dinotopia on the Web at www.dinotopia.com
Visit HarperCollins Children's Books on the Web at
www.harperchildrens.com

Please address letters to the author to:
James Gurney
P.O. Box 391
Red Hook, NY 12571

*D*INOTOPIA, *THE LAND APART FROM TIME, where* humans and dinosaurs coexist in harmony, had been safe for thousands of years. But Will Denison, a skybax rider in training, knew it had not always been so. Long ages ago the empire of Poseidos had threatened to take over Dinotopia and replace the natural world with man-made technology. Fortunately for Dinotopia, it was an age of heroes. One of the heroes was Gideon Altaire, who in his daring attempt to save Dinotopia became the first person ever to fly on the giant pterosaur known as a skybax.

Will Denison owed a debt to Gideon. It was because of Gideon that he was now a skybax rider. And with his last phase of training about to begin, the time had come for Will Denison to read about Gideon and the first flight.

As Will began to read the scroll, the empire of Poseidos arose before him. . . .

Gideon Altaire was late for school again.

He had already missed the skimmer bus, so he caught a ride on the tail of a bronto strutter instead. Gideon's hoverhead, Fritz, floated beside him. Hoverheads were small robots whose multipurpose heads could hover above their bodies. Poor Fritz, though, had no working body. Gideon had rescued him from a garbage strutter a few months ago, and only his head could move about.

"Gideon," squeaked Fritz. "We late." His head zigzagged from side to side. "Roff Stricker very angry." Roff Stricker was in charge of the flight school that Gideon attended, as well as the Strutterworks, a factory that produced machines that looked like animals.

"Ease up, Fritz," said Gideon, "or you'll short your circuits. I've got to program you to quit being so nervous."

As the strutter passed by his school, Gideon jumped off and ran to his classroom, while Fritz joined the other hoverheads.

Fritz tried to salute properly, but without a body it was very difficult to do.

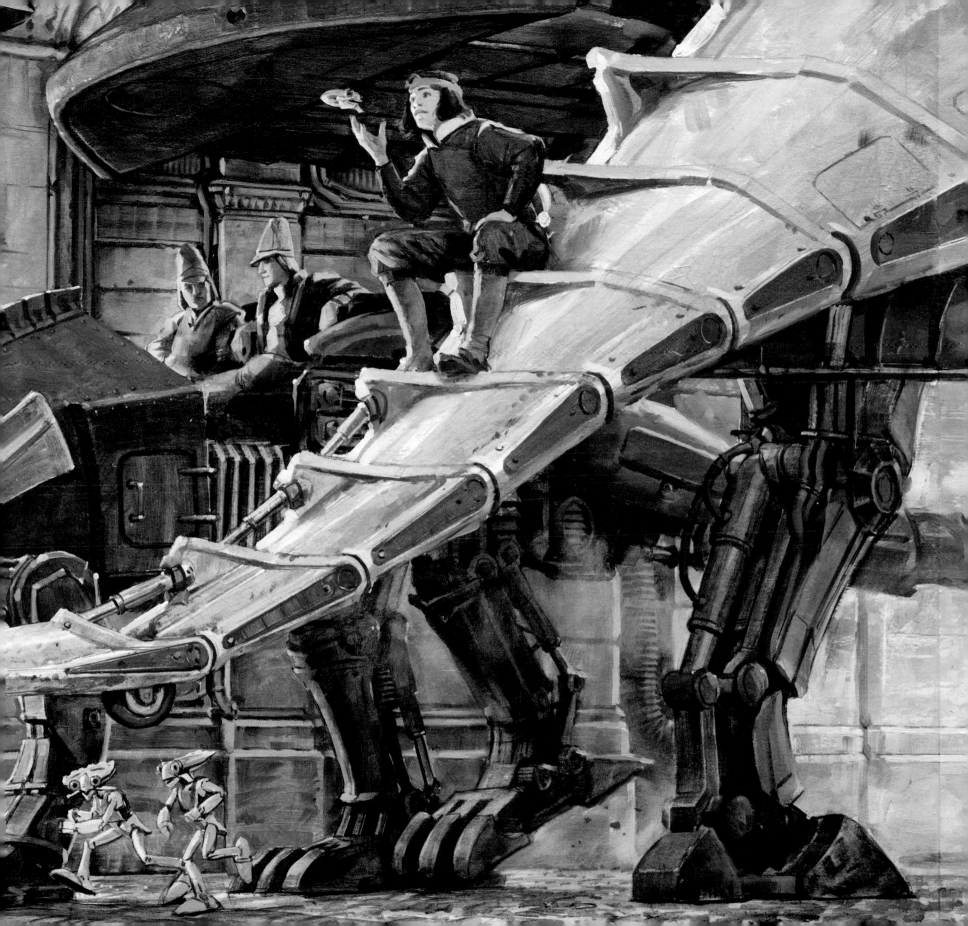

When Gideon arrived at the classroom, he quickly climbed into his flight pod, hoping no one would notice he was late. The students were using their remotely piloted drones to herd captured dinosaurs on Ko Veng Island into an enclosure. But Gideon hated the assignment. He didn't want to control the dinosaurs. He just wanted to watch them.

He landed his drone and leaned back.

A large dinosaur foot came down on the drone, smashing it to pieces.

At once Gideon was summoned into Roff Stricker's office.

"I'm sure you are aware that this is not the first time you have ruined school property," Roff Stricker said. "I do not understand why you keep straying from your assignment."

"I think I need a different assignment," Gideon answered. As an afterthought he added, "Sir." He did not like being lectured.

There was a flicker of anger across Roff Stricker's face.

"Young man," he said coolly, "you've got spirit and you've got talent, and these can be good qualities in a drone pilot. But you need discipline. You need to be a part of the machine, a part of the grand plan." He paused. "I offer you this choice: fit in with us. Follow orders. Make friends. If you do, you could go to the top and be a formation leader. If you do not, I am afraid we cannot hold a place for you here."

"I don't want to fit in with you," Gideon retorted. "I'll find my own friends."

Gideon walked slowly home through the rain-washed streets, with Fritz whirring along beside him. He wasn't sorry for what he had said to Stricker, but he wondered what he was going to do now. Though he hated flight school, he loved the feeling of flying and knew he would miss it.

Gideon was an orphan. He could scarcely remember his parents, who had died years ago. Since then he had drifted about, always feeling out of place. Maybe that's why he and Fritz got along so well. They were both misfits.

Gideon climbed the stairs to his little apartment and went out onto the lookout platform.

Far off to the west he could see the mainland of Dinotopia.

More than anything he wanted to travel to this forbidden world. But by orders of King Ogthar, no Poseidian was allowed to go to the mainland anymore. This was all part of King Ogthar's plan to turn Poseidos into a purely mechanized civilization. Preventing people from visiting the mainland kept them away from the animals there.

Suddenly there was a soft sound behind him. Gideon spun around and found a small creature huddled on the edge of the railing. It was a pterosaur, and it had an injured wing. He reached out a hand to the wet and shivering creature.

"I wonder how you got here," Gideon said.

He knew that no one in Poseidos was allowed to keep an animal, but he decided to bring the pterosaur inside his apartment anyway.

11

Gideon set the pterosaur on his workbench and gently bandaged its wing.

Then he unwrapped some nutrition pellets.

The animal took one of the pellets and immediately spat it out. "I know, I know," Gideon chuckled. "They taste pretty bad, don't they? It's all we get to eat in Poseidos now that they've gotten rid of the plants."

Then Gideon said, "Can you speak? Do you have a name?"

The pterosaur looked suspiciously at Fritz, who was recharging his batteries.

Gideon patted Fritz on the head. "Oh, don't worry about him. He's not like most machines. You can trust him."

The pterosaur nodded and squawked his name, "Razzamult." He looked around Gideon's room and noticed a poster of a dance troupe on the wall and started gesturing at it with his good wing.

"The dance parade?" asked Gideon, puzzled. "Do you want to go there?"

"Yes! Yes!" Razzamult chattered, bobbing up and down excitedly.

Gideon hid Razzamult in a satchel and woke up Fritz. The three of them went off to the dance parade. They stood alongside the parade route and watched as the masked dancers glided past them. First there were women with *Parasaurolophus* masks, then high-stepping stilt walkers in *Brachiosaurus* skeleton costumes. Men with *Triceratops* helmets leaped in the air, followed by *Allosaurus* dancers snapping at their heels. Finally a group of women dressed as *Quetzalcoatlus* swept the air with their wings.

Since live animals had been banned from Poseidos, the performers had had to dress up like dinosaurs, instead of dancing with them as they had once done.

Gideon was inspired by the spectacle.

When the dancers had passed, Razzamult motioned for Gideon to follow after them. They went along many remote streets of the city, through areas Gideon had never seen before, until they reached the dance troupe's camp.

The camp was a cluster of tents surrounding a large balloon ship.

Gideon reasoned that the airship must take the troupe from place to place. At Razzamult's urging, Gideon walked to the airship and climbed into its hull. An old man and a young woman were there.

Razzamult climbed out of the satchel and spoke to the man in a strange language. The old man listened carefully and then said to Gideon, "Please forgive Razzamult for speaking in a language that you don't understand.

"My name is Faldo Mustakka, and this is my niece, Mirella.

"Razzamult tells me he was lost in a storm and that you have helped him."

"Does he belong to you?" asked Gideon curiously.

Faldo laughed. "No, no, he belongs entirely to himself. But he is well-known in Dinotopia as one of the members of Highnest, the roosting place of the pterosaurs."

Faldo continued, "Razzamult just told me that Highnest has been invaded. The ruby sunstone that has been kept there for safekeeping has been stolen away, and four pterosaurs have been taken prisoner here in Poseidos. They are somewhere in the Strutterworks."

"What's the ruby sunstone?" Gideon asked. He knew that sunstones powered the strutters and skimmers in Poseidos, but he had never heard of a ruby sunstone before.

Faldo thought for a moment and then said, "The ruby sunstone is many things to many creatures. In Highnest it safely binds together the energies of good and evil for all of Dinotopia. But away from Highnest it can magnify dark desires. A man or machine with evil intentions can drink enough power from it to destroy all of Dinotopia." Faldo closed his eyes. "Razzamult fears that it has been brought here with such a plan in mind."

Gideon was horrified. "First they get rid of the dinosaurs in Poseidos, and then they get rid of them on the mainland," he said. "That's why Stricker was making us practice herding dinosaurs at flight school."

Faldo nodded. "Razzamult says he thinks you are the hero we need to get the sunstone back."

"Me? A hero?" said Gideon, startled. "I just got kicked out of flight school. All the students there say that I'm a lightweight."

"Lightweights fly higher," Faldo said, smiling.

Gideon thought for a moment. He had no ties to Poseidos, and this might be his best chance to get to the mainland. "I'll do it. But this could be dangerous."

"Razzamult will join you for now," responded Faldo. "You will find others later. Here. Let me offer you this small gift before you go." The old man handed Gideon a conch shell. "Blow on this shell when you are in danger, and friends will come to help you."

"I can use all the help I can get," said Gideon. "Can I try it out?" He lifted it to his mouth, but only succeeded in making a feeble squeak. Mirella couldn't help giggling.

Gideon turned to her and muttered, "And who are *you* supposed to be, the blue fairy?"

"No, just someone who can help you look more heroic." She opened a trunk and brought out the uniform of a guard from the Strutterworks.

"Put this on and you'll look more official," she said.

After Gideon put on the costume, he and Fritz left the camp. Razzamult was able to fit inside Gideon's hat. But as they approached the Strutterworks, Gideon realized that he was going to be in big trouble. As was the custom in Poseidos, the guards saluted each other by raising their hats.

But Gideon couldn't lift his hat properly with Razzamult hidden inside.

Thinking fast, Gideon distracted the guards by telling them he needed to get his hoverhead fixed. The guards let him pass.

The three companions were safely inside the building. They entered a series of corridors that led them farther and farther into the Strutterworks, until they reached a large hangar.

There lay a giant air scorpion.

It was the largest machine Gideon had ever seen. In its back were dozens of launch bays for flying drones. Gideon realized that this was the ship that could conquer the mainland, just as Razzamult had warned.

Fritz started beeping for Gideon to approach the cockpit of the air scorpion. There, in the power unit of the ship just above the cockpit, was the ruby sunstone. It hummed and crackled with power. When Gideon reached out to grab it, it sent sharp jolts of energy through his body and made him feel dizzy. With a great effort he managed to slip it into a pouch on his belt.

Instantly an alarm sounded. Fritz inserted a probe into a control panel and shifted the alarm to a different part of the building. Gideon knew he had only minutes before he would be caught.

He brought the conch shell to his lips and trumpeted out a clear, loud sound. Immediately he heard the cries of the captured pterosaurs in response. They were in a room nearby! The door to the room was locked, but Gideon kicked in a grille and crawled into a ventilation duct. He slid down and down.

Gideon was trapped in a wind tunnel.

A huge propeller pulled the air through the room, creating enough wind to keep the pterosaurs aloft. Gideon realized that this wind tunnel was where the engineers observed living creatures to help them design man-made replacements.

Razzamult sprang to Gideon's hand and called to the other pterosaurs, "Catapult! Scimitar! Zanzibar! Avatar!" The four pterosaurs screeched back in turn. Avatar, the largest of them, flew close to Gideon and met his eyes. Gideon was awestruck. He had no idea that a flying creature could be so big. He dreamed of seeing them all flying free.

The sound of an air lock opening interrupted Gideon's thoughts. There stood Roff Stricker. He snarled, "So, Gideon. I see you have found some new friends. And look where they've landed you! I'll give you a choice, which is more than you deserve. Just give me back my ruby sunstone, and I'll let you return to flight school. Refuse, and you'll never see these pterosaurs again."

Gideon was trembling. He could feel his heart pounding. But he found the courage to say, "The ruby sunstone isn't yours, and neither are the pterosaurs!" He quickly scanned the wind tunnel. A few feet away was a big side portal. Gideon dove toward it and managed to wrestle it open. He was free, and so were the pterosaurs!

23

Gideon held Razzamult as the other pterosaurs escaped into the sky. He then ran across the rooftops to a skimmer landing. Luck was with him. There was a yellow police skimmer waiting. He plunged the ruby sunstone into the power unit while Fritz started up the antigravity generator. Gideon jammed the control handles forward just in time to escape his pursuers, who came from every direction.

He raced the skimmer through back alleys and busy traffic.

He shot out past the fish fleet and away from Poseidos.
His skimmer was incredibly fast, but it didn't steer well.

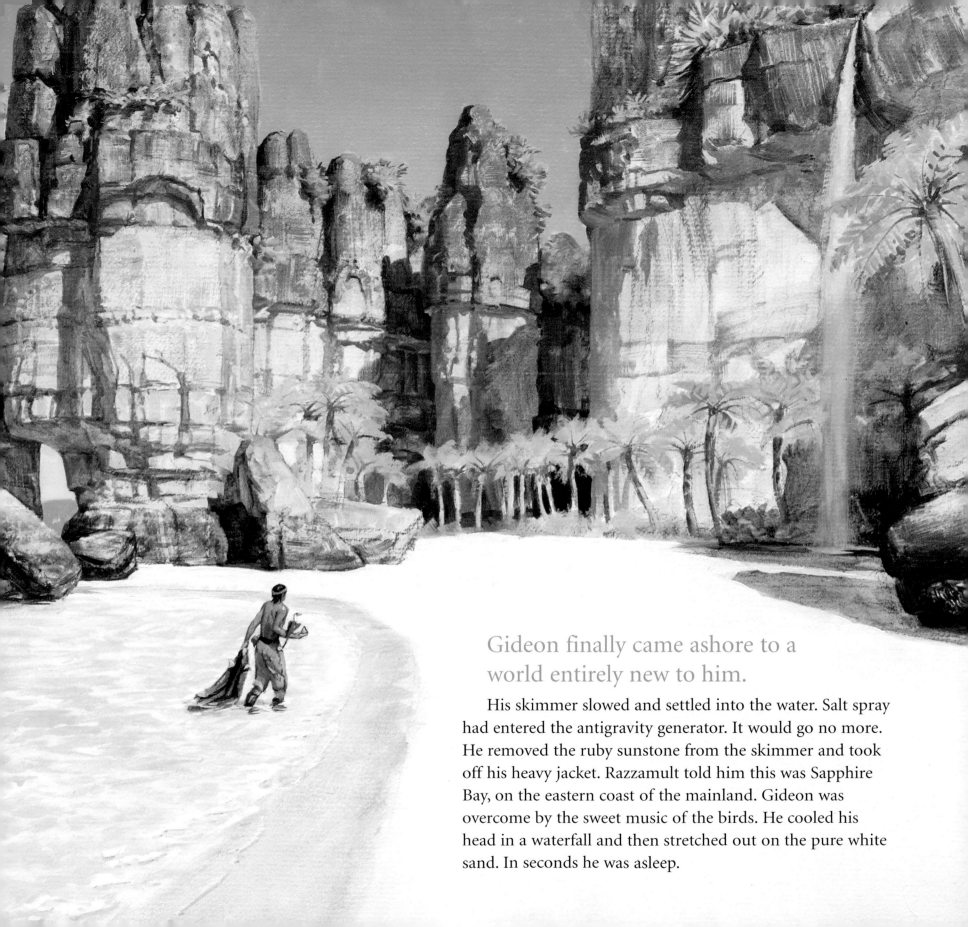

Gideon finally came ashore to a world entirely new to him.

His skimmer slowed and settled into the water. Salt spray had entered the antigravity generator. It would go no more. He removed the ruby sunstone from the skimmer and took off his heavy jacket. Razzamult told him this was Sapphire Bay, on the eastern coast of the mainland. Gideon was overcome by the sweet music of the birds. He cooled his head in a waterfall and then stretched out on the pure white sand. In seconds he was asleep.

GIDEON AWOKE REFRESHED. But when he got up, he realized he was not alone. A group of people and dinosaurs had gathered around him, viewing him in silence.

Finally a *Triceratops* said, "You are too young to be a guard from Poseidos. Who are you really? And why are you here?"

Gideon told them his name and explained how he had arrived on their shore.

Razzamult then informed them about the ruby sunstone. At the sight of it they welcomed the companions heartily with a feast of seafood and fruit. They even accepted Fritz after they saw him trying to park his head on some bottles and a guitar—on anything that looked like a body. They agreed that machines can be loyal friends once they become a little old and rusty.

During the meal, the *Triceratops*, whose name was Humadee, and a ring-tailed *Plesictis* named Bandy told Gideon about a rumor that fighter sprogs were going to invade the coastline of Dinotopia. Sprogs were cruel strutters that had legs like a spider's, eyes like a frog's, and bellies like prison cells.

"We have no time to lose!" declared Gideon. "I know Stricker won't give up even with the air scorpion grounded. Razzamult, can you fly to Highnest to tell the pterosaurs I'm on my way?" Razzamult, whose wing was almost better, flew off at once.

Fritz had been darting to and fro, saying good-bye to their new friends. Suddenly he started circling around Gideon's head. "Sprogs! Sprogs! Run! Run!" he beeped frantically.

While they had been talking, the fish fleet had come ashore bearing a cargo of fighter sprogs.

Humadee said to Gideon, "You and Bandy run into the Mukkawukka Swamp. Bandy can lead you to Highnest from there. We'll divert the sprogs. Now go!"

Gideon hated abandoning them to the sprogs, but he knew that delivering the ruby sunstone was the only way he could save them all.

He followed Bandy, who darted ahead through the thick forest shouting, "This way! This way!"

At times they thought they heard sprogs in the distance. Gideon blew on the shell trumpet. They needed more help. Soon there was a rustling in the bushes, and three more creatures appeared.

Budge

Latin name: ESTEMMENOSUCHUS
(eh-STEM-en-uh-SOOK-us),
a mammal-like reptile; male
Size: 4 feet 8 inches long
Favorite food: water plants
Special abilities: biting hard and holding on

Binny

Latin name: NECROLEMUR
(NECK-row-lee-mur), a relative of
the modern tarsier; female
Size: 20 inches long, including tail
Favorite food: tough-shelled insects
Special abilities: excellent vision,
flute playing, and leaping
Special tool: combination vine snipper,
pruning saw, and flute

Bandy

Latin name: PLESICTIS (please-ICT-iss), ancestor of the cacomistle; female
Size: 2 feet 5 inches long, including tail
Favorite food: berries and insects
Special abilities: superb hearing
Special tool: fig flinger can launch berries and nuts at any target within 50 feet

Bongo

Latin name: PLESIADAPIS (please-ee-uh-DAPE-iss), monkey family; male
Size: 3 feet 9 inches long, including tail
Favorite food: frogs and nuts
Special abilities: rock climbing, lassooing, keen sense of smell
Backpack tool kit: includes hammer, grappling hook, and rope

"What's up?" asked Bongo, when they had all introduced themselves.

Gideon showed them the ruby sunstone and told them of his goal to return it to Highnest.

Bongo scratched his chin. "Well, it ain't going to be no picnic getting up there," he said. "Not unless you got wings. The way you're headed, there's crocs bigger than tyrannosaurs. They'll bite you in half."

"They don't scare me," snorted Budge. "I'll bite them back."

"Are you implying I'm scared?" Bongo said. "Because if you are, let me tell you—"

"Friends, friends," interrupted Binny. "Stop arguing. This is really important."

"She's right," said Bandy. "We need to work together. Once they finish with Highnest, they'll come after Mukkawukka Swamp next. Let's go to Highnest!"

The four animals raised up a cheer. Then Binny handed out crunchy grasshoppers to celebrate their decision to help Gideon. To be polite, Gideon pretended to take a bite of one and then discreetly dropped it behind a plant.

Binny also offered a grasshopper to Fritz, who was beginning to run low on power.

"No thanks, please," Fritz whined. "Need real food. Recharge. Big jolt." He dropped to the ground.

"Come here," said Gideon kindly. He picked up Fritz and set him on the ruby sunstone for a few minutes. "Now, don't let it go to your head."

Fritz spiraled upward, fully recharged.

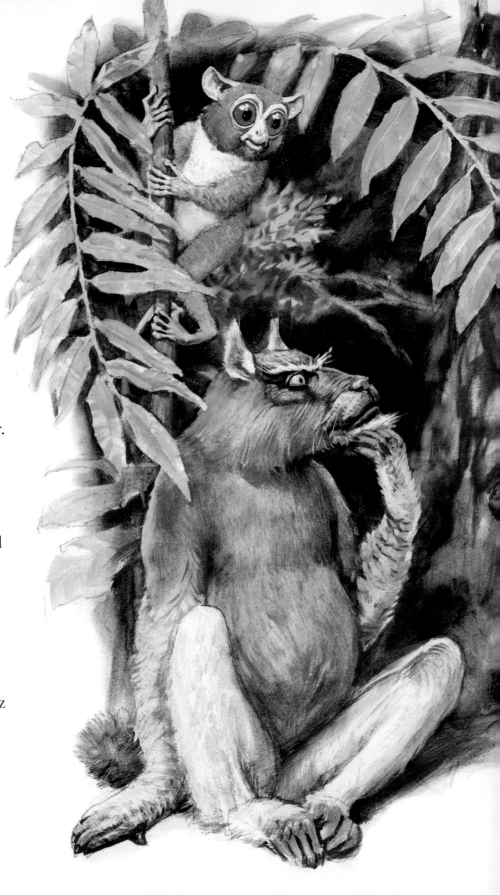

The companions continued on their journey. Soon they came to a wide and murky river. The only crossing was over a fallen tree, beneath which lurked a *Deinosuchus*.

The giant crocodile spent his day waiting for someone to slip off the log.

Binny crossed in two big jumps. She played a slow song on her flute that hypnotized the crocodile. Bandy and Bongo crossed safely, followed by Budge, who growled deep in this throat. But the growl must have awakened the crocodile, for just as Gideon was halfway over, the beast reared up against the log. Gideon lost his footing and fell right onto the crocodile's back.

"Throw me a rope, Bongo!" he yelled.

Budge bit down on one end of the rope to secure it and Bongo threw it. Gideon caught the other end and was pulled to safety.

"Thanks, guys!" Gideon said. "I was almost breakfast back there."

Gideon and his friends were now
deep in the Mukkawukka Swamp.

They tiptoed along a line of half-submerged logs
until they came into a dense part of the jungle where
thick plants screened the way ahead. The little motors
in Fritz's head made a nervous, whining sound.

"I smell something," said Bongo.

"I hear something," said Bandy.

"I see something," said Binny. "It's a sprog!"

"Let me at it. I just want to taste it!" said Budge.

But it was too late. Before they could jump out of
the way, the sprog's door blew open and a net shot out.
The animals dodged the net and stayed just out of its
reach, but Gideon was captured.

Two red hoverheads climbed out of
the hatch and snickered at Gideon.

One took the sunstone out of Gideon's pouch.
He placed it on top of his metallic head. The head flew
straight up and away. The other hoverhead brought
Gideon inside the sprog.

41

The mouth of the sprog clanked shut. Gideon was trapped.

But the hero partners were ready. They pounced on the sprog.

A claw grabbed Bandy. Binny jumped up and sliced through the control cables to set Bandy free. Budge chomped through the pressure hoses in the sprog's legs, releasing clouds of steam. The sprog staggered.

Meanwhile, Fritz and Bongo popped open the roof hatch and freed Gideon. The three of them neutralized all the hoverheads.

Gideon attached Fritz to one of the hoverheads' bodies. The fit was perfect. "Finally!" said Gideon. "A hoverhead with a good head on his shoulders."

Fritz stumbled around. He touched his face with his new fingertips and then awkwardly saluted. "All better now, boss. Ready to help!"

"How can any of us help now?" mused Gideon, now that the flush of victory was over. "We've lost the sunstone. We've failed. Highnest is in more danger than ever."

"All the more reason to go," said Budge.

They began the climb toward Highnest.

Razzamult
Scaphognathus

Fritz
Caputvolens

Binny
Necrolemur

Catapult
Tapejara

Bandy
Plesictis

Highnest seemed to float above the clouds like a mirage, but it was solid stone, shaped by wind and rain to create a fortified rookery for the pterosaurs. The companions paused long enough to behold it from Rainbow Arch. There they were met by a flock of pterosaurs, led by the four that Gideon had freed from the wind tunnel.

But the welcome was brief. Gideon told them about the sprog invasion and the loss of the ruby sunstone. There wasn't much time. By now the sunstone was back in the air scorpion. Highnest would be the first target. Stricker could control the skies only if he could conquer the pterosaurs. They would have to fight Stricker in the air.

But first they had to save the pterosaur eggs.

The hero partners and the pterosaurs joined forces, and soon the eggs were in a safe location deep in the canyons beyond Highnest.

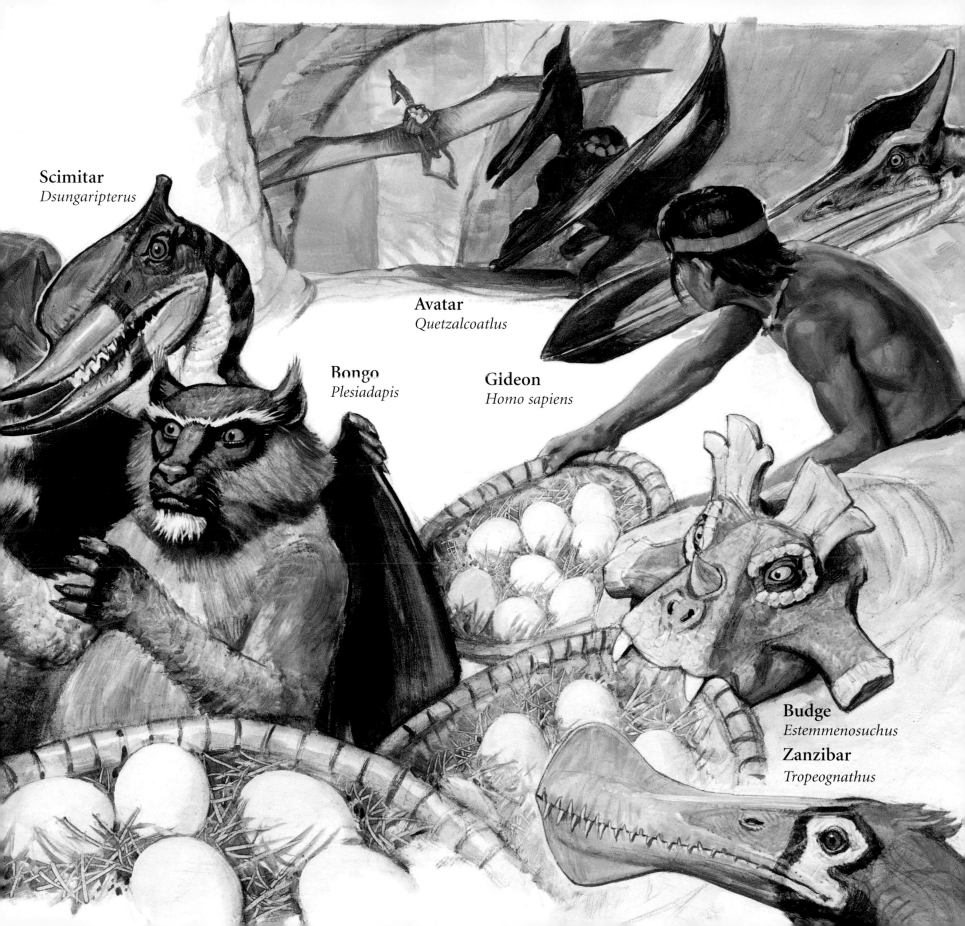

Scimitar
Dsungaripterus

Avatar
Quetzalcoatlus

Bongo
Plesiadapis

Gideon
Homo sapiens

Budge
Estemmenosuchus

Zanzibar
Tropeognathus

With the eggs safely hidden, the pterosaurs returned to the hero partners, who were waiting on a balcony at Highnest. Gideon peered off into the clouds.

"If only I had a skimmer," he said. "I could fly out there and see if the air scorpion has left Poseidos."

"If only I was higher up, I could *see* Poseidos from here," said Binny.

"And I could hear it," said Bandy.

"I can smell Poseidos, anyhow," grumbled Bongo.

Fritz urgently tapped on Gideon's shoulder. "Excuse me, please," he said. "Razzamult has idea for you."

The pterosaurs had been in a huddle, chattering with each other excitedly. Razzamult hushed them and said to the hero partners, "You don't look much heavier than the eggs we just carried. And you are just as precious to us now. If you wish to fly, we will take you aloft."

"Us? Now? You could, really?" Gideon said, almost speechless with enthusiasm.

Razzamult said nothing more, but spread his wings

and stood close to Binny. Her eyes sparkled with
excitement as she leaped lightly onto his back.
Catapult was next, calling to Bandy with a raucous
clacking that Bandy answered with a friendly growl.

Bongo and Budge whooped as they swung
themselves aboard Scimitar and Zanzibar.

Only Avatar was left. He embraced Gideon with
his huge wings. Then he tilted his head back and
screeched. Gideon climbed aboard and then turned
to Fritz, who stood alone with his knees shaking.

"Come on, Fritz," Gideon said. "You're not afraid,
are you?" He offered a hand and hoisted him aboard.
"Just hold on to me."

They launched off the edge of the
cliff and circled upward.

Gideon had never experienced anything like this
before. Flying a skimmer or a drone was nothing like
being on the back of a living, breathing creature.

During their flight they saw nothing of the air
scorpion. It had already left Poseidos and was skimming
across the water, far below the clouds. Gideon and his
friends returned to Highnest to find it already beginning
its attack. Drones were pouring out of its back and
flying into the honeycombed interior of Highnest.

"Partners!" shouted Gideon. "We've got to stop
them!" It made him angry to think that these drones
were probably piloted remotely by the same students
in the flight school who used to call him names.

"Take that!" he yelled, as he
smacked a drone and sent it
crashing out of control.

The small band of heroes flew directly toward the air scorpion. The drones fired shock pulses that nearly knocked the riders from their pterosaurs.

One of the scorpion's giant claws reached out for Gideon and snatched him off Avatar.

The claw brought him near enough to the windshield to see that Roff Stricker was piloting it alone inside. Stricker's voice boomed from a speaker.

"You're finished, Gideon. Your time is up."

"You can't stop us all!"
Gideon shouted.

Budge chomped through the hoses that controlled the scorpion's claw, loosening its grip on Gideon, who wriggled free and climbed up the scorpion's arm toward the cockpit. Bandy used her fig flinger to launch one juicy fig after another squarely onto the windshield, blocking Stricker's view ahead. Bongo scrambled to the ruby sunstone and tried to pull it loose, but he was thrown back by the energy it emitted.

Meanwhile Binny cut the wires in the air scorpion that carried signals to the drones. The drones plummeted to earth and exploded. Then Fritz changed the balance controls, and the scorpion went into a tailspin. Finally Gideon himself reached the ruby sunstone, and with a great effort, pulled it loose. All this time the pterosaurs had been flying close by.

Seconds before impact, the hero partners jumped off the air scorpion and were saved by the pterosaurs.

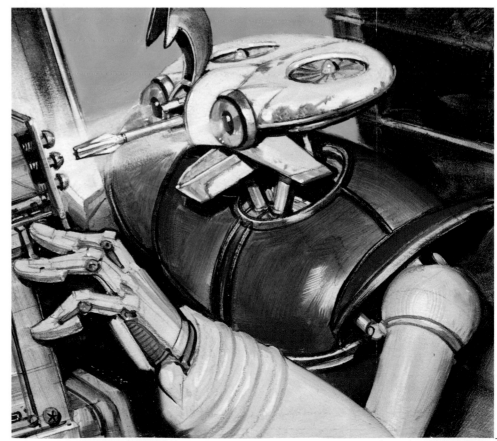

The air scorpion crashed to the ground in a ball of flame. Just before it hit, Gideon saw the cockpit hatch pop open. A small skimmer shot out and headed back to Poseidos.

The partners returned to Highnest, exhausted but happy. The eggs were brought back to their nests, and Gideon replaced the sunstone. All the animals shouted together, "Hooray for Gideon, hero of Highnest!"

"We couldn't have done it without each other," he replied modestly.

Later that day Avatar pulled Gideon aside. He presented Gideon with a clay tablet that he had scratched out with his own claw. It was a token of thanks for all Gideon had done to save Highnest, and a symbol of the bond that they had created by flying together.

Gideon held Avatar's token as they watched the sun pass behind the curve of the earth.

Will Denison read the last few sentences of the scroll again. He rolled up the scroll and blew out his lantern. The hour was late. The rumble of Waterfall City was calling him to bed.

As he rose out of the chair, he heard a sound at the open window. It was Cirrus, Will's skybax. Cirrus stretched out his claw and handed something heavy to Will. Even in the dim light Will knew what he had been given. It was a token that Cirrus had carved for Will, the symbol of the bond between skybax and rider that had been forged on the first flight.